The Magical Animal Fairies

Special thanks to
Narinder Dhami

ORCHARD BOOKS
338 Euston Road, London NW1 3BH
Orchard Books Australia
Level 17/207 Kent Street, Sydney, NSW 2000
A Paperback Original

First published in 2009 by Orchard Books.

© 2009 Rainbow Magic Limited.
A HIT Entertainment company. Rainbow Magic
is a trademark of Rainbow Magic Limited.
Reg. U.S. Pat. & Tm. Off. And other countries.

HiT entertainment

Illustrations © Orchard Books 2009

A CIP catalogue record for this book is available
from the British Library.

ISBN 978 1 40830 350 4
7 9 10 8

Printed in Great Britain

Orchard Books is a division of Hachette Children's Books,
an Hachette UK company

www.hachette.co.uk

Lara
the Black Cat
Fairy

by Daisy Meadows

ORCHARD BOOKS

www.rainbowmagic.co.uk

The Fairyland Palace

Barn

Farmhouse

Stables

Clubhouse

CAMP

Adventure Lake

Birdwatching Tower

There are seven special animals
Who live in Fairyland.
They use their magic powers
To help others where they can.

A dragon, black cat, firebird,
A seahorse and snow swan too,
A unicorn and ice bear -
I know just what to do.

I'll lock them in my castle
And never let them out.
The world will turn more miserable,
Of that, I have no doubt...

Contents

North, South, East, West

"Come on, Kirsty." Rachel Walker picked up her rucksack and smiled at her best friend, Kirsty Tate. "It's time for our next activity – we're going on an orienteering expedition."

"Oh, great!" Kirsty exclaimed happily, lacing up her walking boots. "I'm really looking forward to it." Then she grinned.

"To be honest, I'm not exactly sure what an orienteering expedition is, though!"

Rachel and the other girls in the cabin, Emma, Natasha, Katie and Catherine, smiled warmly at Kirsty.

"Orienteering is using a compass and a map to find your way to a meeting-place," Emma explained. "All the different teams try to get there first. It's great fun."

"It sounds fantastic," Kirsty agreed.

"I've enjoyed every activity here at camp so far," Rachel remarked to Kirsty, as their room-mates went outside.

Kirsty nodded. "And it's been even *more* exciting since our fairy friends asked for our help!" she whispered.

On the day the girls arrived at the camp, they discovered that Jack Frost had been up to his old tricks in Fairyland again. This time he and his naughty goblin servants had kidnapped seven Magical Animals from the Magical Animal Fairies.

The Magical Animals were very rare and precious because they helped to spread the kind of magic that every human and fairy could possess – the magic of imagination, luck, humour, friendship, compassion, healing and courage. The fairies trained the Magical Animals for a whole year to make sure they knew how to use their powers to spread their wonderful gifts throughout the human and the fairy worlds.

But Jack Frost was determined to make sure that the animals never got the chance to use their magical gifts. He wanted everyone to be as grumpy and miserable as him! So he and his goblins had stolen the young Magical Animals and taken them to his Ice Castle. But the animals had managed to escape into the

human world, where they had hidden themselves away. Jack Frost had sent his goblins after them, but Rachel and Kirsty, with the help of the Magical Animal Fairies, were determined to find the young animals first, and return them safely to Fairyland.

"I'm glad we managed to find Sizzle the dragon yesterday," Rachel said, as she and Kirsty left the cabin. "Ashley was so pleased to see him again, wasn't she?"

Kirsty nodded. "I hope we find the other youngsters soon," she said anxiously.

"Remember what the fairies told us — that the Magical Animals can't always control their powers properly because their training isn't finished yet."

"They ran rings around Jack Frost and his goblins when they escaped from the Ice Castle though, didn't they?" Rachel laughed.

Rachel and Kirsty joined their room-mates, who were standing with the girls

from the cabin next door. Edward, one of the camp counsellors, was there too.

"Ah, there you are," Edward said, smiling at Rachel

and Kirsty. "Here's your map and compass. Now, you're all going to walk due west for twenty-seven paces, and find your way to a mystery location!"

Everyone listened carefully as Edward explained how to place the compass on the map and watch the magnetic needle to find out which direction was north.

"Hold the map steady, Kirsty," said Rachel as the needle swung round.

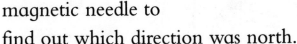

"Look, that's north."

"So west is *that* way," Kirsty said, pointing to her left. "Come on, Rachel!"

Some of the other campers had already headed in that direction, and Rachel and Kirsty followed them, counting their steps under their breath.

"Twenty-four, twenty-five," Rachel murmured. Then she stopped and burst out laughing. "Look, Kirsty, we've arrived at the camp canteen!"

"Well done, everyone," called Edward, who hurried out of the canteen at that moment. He began handing out bottles of water and cereal bars. "That was easy, wasn't it? Now we're going into the fields to try a longer route, so follow me!"

Edward strode off and everyone hurried after him. Soon they were out in the fields that surrounded the camp.

"In orienteering, it's really important to use your compass correctly," Edward explained, opening the gate into the field. "Because this is a race between different teams, you must find the shortest route between the points on your map. If you don't, you won't win!"

"I'm enjoying this, aren't you, Rachel?" Kirsty remarked, taking a sip of water. "I never thought maps and compasses could be so much fun!"

Rachel was about to reply when a soft, muffled noise suddenly caught her attention. She stopped and cocked her head to one side. *Meow!* There it was again!

"I can hear a cat," Kirsty said, glancing around at the long grass.

"Me too," Catherine agreed.

Suddenly Rachel noticed a tiny, jet-black cat in a patch of fuzzy dandelion clocks. The cat was batting at the plants and then chasing the downy white seedlings as they floated off into the air.

"Look, there it is," she pointed out. "Isn't it cute? I wonder where it's come from?"

"It's probably from one of the nearby farms," Edward replied.

"Oh, I love cats," Emma said eagerly. She knelt down on the grass and held out her hand. "Here, kitty!" she cooed.

The cat stopped playing and looked over at them. She had beautiful, emerald-green eyes and her black fur gleamed in the sunshine. As the cat began to purr loudly, Kirsty gave a gasp.

"Rachel!" she whispered. "The cat's whiskers are shimmering!"

"I know, I can see it too!" Rachel murmured, her heart thumping with excitement. "It must be fairy magic!"

Before the girls could say anything more, Rachel suddenly felt her golden locket slip from her neck. She made a grab for it but missed, and it fell into a shallow ditch at her feet.

"Is it broken?" asked Kirsty as Rachel bent to pick it up.

Rachel examined the locket and shook her head. "No, it must have come undone, somehow," she replied, frowning.

A loud flapping of wings overhead made everyone look up at that moment. A large pigeon was swooping down towards them, its bright eyes fixed on the half-eaten cereal bar in Catherine's hand.

"Help!" Catherine shrieked in alarm, as the pigeon grabbed the bar and flew off with it.

"Are you OK, Catherine?" asked Rachel. Before Catherine could reply, Emma, who was still kneeling near the cat, gave a cry of pain.

"Oh, my hand's burning!" she gasped, rubbing it hard. "I must have touched that patch of stinging nettles *there* –"

And she pointed to a patch of nettles. "But I don't remember seeing them before!"

"Here." Edward grabbed a handful of large leaves and passed them to Emma. "Rub these dock leaves where it hurts, and it will feel better."

"Rachel, have you noticed that *three* unlucky things have happened in just one minute?" Kirsty whispered to her friend. "This little black cat *must* be one of the missing Magical Animals!"

Buttercup Surprise

Rachel nodded.

"We know that one of the missing Magical Animals is a black cat who is being trained to spread good luck," she agreed. "And we also know that because the animals are so young, their magic is very unpredictable."

"In this case, it's working in *reverse*!" Kirsty murmured. "We're getting bad luck instead of good luck!"

"We'd better take the cat back to
Fairyland before any goblins appear,"
said Rachel. She turned to glance at
the cat again, but at that very moment
it bounded away through a patch of
silky red poppies. Rachel and Kirsty
shared a glance of dismay.

"OK, that little cat's got the right idea!" Edward announced, clapping his hands. "Let's get a move on."

"At least Edward and the other girls haven't noticed anything out of the ordinary about the cat," Kirsty whispered, relieved. "They think it's just a farm cat."

Meanwhile, Edward had begun dividing the girls into teams of two.

"Rachel and Kirsty, you're a team," he said, handing them an envelope.

"Oh, that's good!" Rachel exclaimed in a low voice, grinning at Kirsty. "We'll be able to keep a look-out for the cat."

"Yes, maybe we're getting some *good* luck too!" Kirsty pointed out.

"Right, each team has a different set of instructions inside their envelope," Edward explained. "The clues will lead you all around the fields, but if you have any problems, I'll be close by at all times." He glanced at his watch. "It's midday now and we should aim to meet at 12.30. All the instructions will lead you to the same place, where there'll be a surprise waiting for you! Good luck!"

28

"I wonder what the surprise is?" Kirsty remarked, tearing open the envelope. She unfolded the instructions and read aloud: "'Head north through the field for sixty paces until you reach a fence. Then turn right (due east). Follow the fence for ten paces  until you reach a wooden gate.'"

"That doesn't seem too difficult," Rachel said, as the other teams began to hurry off in different directions. "Maybe we'll spot the cat again while we're following the instructions!"

"I hope so," Kirsty replied.

Carefully, the girls lined up the compass and began to walk in a northerly direction, counting their steps. As they walked, they both kept looking around the field, but there was no sign of the little black cat.

"Twenty-one, twenty-two," Kirsty murmured. Then she stopped. "Rachel, was it fifty or sixty paces to the north?"

"I can't remember." Rachel shook her head. "Check the paper, Kirsty."

Kirsty unfolded the instructions again. Then she let out a gasp.

"Rachel, look!" she cried. "The writing has changed – and so have the directions!"

The girls stared at the paper. "Head west for forty strides until you find a cluster of glimmering buttercups" was written in swirly golden letters.

"Fairy magic!" Rachel gasped. "It must be! Quick, Kirsty, which way is west?"

Trembling with excitement, Kirsty consulted the compass.

"That way!" she said, pointing across the field.

The girls hurried west, counting their paces as they went.

"Look at that golden light!" Kirsty pointed just ahead of them after they'd gone thirty-eight paces. "That must be the patch of buttercups glimmering in the sun."

"I wonder what we'll find there?" Rachel said eagerly.

The golden heads of the buttercups were nodding and dancing in the warm breeze. Rachel and Kirsty bent over the flowers, peering down at them. Suddenly Rachel clutched Kirsty's arm.

"Look, Kirsty!" she exclaimed. "Right there in the middle of all the buttercups!"

Kirsty looked where Rachel was pointing and saw a tiny fairy perched on a buttercup, waving up at them.

"It's Lara the Black Cat Fairy!" Kirsty cried.

A Trail of Clover

Looking very pleased to see them, Lara fluttered up out of the buttercups. She wore a silver cardigan, jeans, black buckled boots and a scarf printed with little cats. Her long, shiny black hair swirled around her as she flew to land gracefully on Kirsty's shoulder.

"Hello, girls," Lara said with a big smile. "I'm so glad you received my message! I'm looking for my little black cat, Lucky. I just know she's close by!"

"We saw her a few moments ago, Lara," Rachel explained quickly, "playing in a patch of dandelion clocks."

"But she ran away before we could catch her," Kirsty added.

Lara nodded. "We *must* find her before Jack Frost's goblins do," she said anxiously. "We'd better search the fields. Which way do you think we should go first, girls?"

Rachel and Kirsty glanced about. The other teams had scattered now, and there was no one else around.

"Maybe we'd better go back to the dandelion clocks and start from there," Kirsty suggested.

Rachel was about to agree, when at that moment she looked down and noticed something that made her eyes open wide with surprise. There, nestling in the grass at her feet, was a four-leaf clover. Rachel stared down at it, excitement flooding through her. She'd heard about lucky four-leaf clovers before, although she'd never seen one, as they were very rare.

But then Rachel blinked in surprise as she noticed *another* four-leaf clover a little way ahead of her, and then another, and another!

"Look!" Rachel gasped, kneeling down and pointing at the little plant right in front of her. "I think I've found a trail of four-leaf clovers!"

"Wow!" Kirsty gasped. "I've never even seen *one* before – let alone a whole trail!"

Lara was clapping her hands in delight. "Lucky has left this trail!" she declared. "We *must* follow it immediately!"

Quickly, Rachel and Kirsty began to follow the winding trail of four-leaf clovers. They were easy to spot amongst the grass because they shimmered slightly with fairy magic.

"The trail seems to be leading us in the direction of that farmyard over there," Kirsty said, pointing ahead of them.

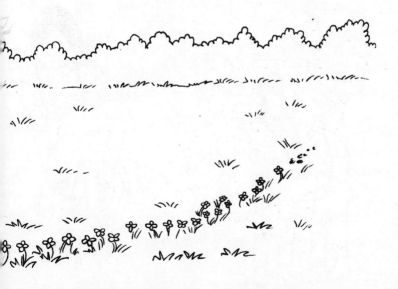

The farmyard looked very quiet and there was no one around – just a few geese waddling about. Lara and the girls could also see a big barn and three haystacks.

"The trail's stopped," Lara said with a frown, pausing at the edge of the farmyard. "But Lucky's still around here somewhere. I can definitely sense that she's close by!"

"Let's search the farmyard," Kirsty suggested, glancing at Rachel. But her friend was frowning and looking rather perplexed.

"What's the matter, Rachel?" asked Kirsty.

"Well, I'm sure that there were *three* haystacks in the farmyard a moment ago," Rachel replied. "But look." She pointed across the yard. "Now there are only two!"

Kirsty and Lara stared at the haystacks. Rachel was right. There were now only two of them.

"That's strange –" Kirsty began.

Suddenly they all heard a tiny *meow*.

The next moment, a small black cat
bounded across the farmyard, chasing
a leaf that danced
in the breeze.

"Lucky!" Lara gasped.

Lucky stopped in front of one of
the haystacks and cocked her head
eagerly at the sound of Lara's voice.

"Lucky!" Lara called again.

At that very moment a long green
nose poked out of the middle of the
biggest haystack. Then a second
nose poked out of the other one.

Rachel, Kirsty and Lara watched in horror as first one pair of green arms, and then another, popped out of each side of both the haystacks.

"Goblins!" Kirsty exclaimed. "They're hiding in the haystacks!"

As Lucky turned to run towards Lara, the goblins leapt out of the haystacks. One of them grabbed Lucky, who mewed and wriggled, but couldn't get away. Then, chuckling triumphantly, the goblins scurried off across the farmyard.

"After them!" Lara cried.

Three Against Three

Immediately, Kirsty and Rachel ran after the goblins, with Lara flying alongside them. But as they dashed across the farmyard, the third haystack suddenly appeared from around the corner of the farmhouse. It stopped in front of them, blocking their path.

"Oh no!" Rachel groaned, skidding to a halt. "That's the other haystack!"

"Haystacks don't move on their own," Kirsty gasped. "There's a goblin inside!"

"Don't despair, girls!" Lara declared, flicking her wand and sending fairy sparkles dancing around them. "We'll *fly* over it!"

Instantly, Kirsty and Rachel shrank down to become as tiny as Lara, with gossamer-thin wings on their backs. All three of them whizzed up into the air and flew over the top of the haystack.

"Not fair!" the goblin inside shouted grumpily in a muffled voice.

Rachel glanced back over her shoulder. "He's coming after us," she warned, as the goblin shook himself free of the haystack and charged across the farmyard behind them.

"I think those other two goblins are heading for the barn," Kirsty panted.

The three friends flew as fast as they could and soon began to catch up with the two goblins in front of them.

Then, suddenly, the goblin holding
Lucky gave a loud roar of surprise as he
tripped over a milk pail lying on its side
in the middle of the farmyard. The pail
flew up into the air and landed neatly
over the goblin's head!

"Help!" he shouted,
staggering about.
"Who turned
out the lights?"

"This might
be our chance to
grab Lucky!" Lara
whispered to Kirsty
and Rachel.

But the other goblin was too quick for
them. Leaving his friend stuck in the
milk pail, he grabbed the little black cat
from him, and rushed towards the barn.

But he didn't notice a patch of grain
lying on the floor near the barn door.
He slipped and landed
on his bottom with
a shriek, letting
go of Lucky.

"The goblins
are having lots of
bad luck!" Rachel
whispered, as she, Lara
and Kirsty swooped down towards him.
"Let's grab Lucky and get out of here!"

But before they could reach the little
cat, the other goblin finally pulled the
milk pail from his head. He darted
towards the barn, scooped up Lucky and
ran inside, slamming the heavy door shut
behind him. Meanwhile, the other goblin
was still sitting on the ground, groaning.

"Look out!" shouted the third goblin, who was chasing after Lara, Kirsty and Rachel. "Pesky fairies!"

The goblin who had slipped glanced up and shrieked with rage. He jumped to his feet and began hitting out at Lara and the girls as they hovered near the barn door. "We have to find a way into the barn!" Lara said urgently as both goblins leapt up and down, trying to knock them out of the air.

"Let's take a look around," Kirsty suggested, neatly dodging the goblins' big green hands.

Lara, Rachel and Kirsty slowly circled the barn, keeping well out of reach of the two goblins below.

"Look, there's a crack in the wall!" Rachel said eagerly. "Do you think it's big enough for us to get through?"

"Sure it is!" Lara grinned. "Come on!"

She flew forward and slipped through the crack. Rachel and Kirsty followed.

The barn was full of sacks of animal feed and farmyard tools. Kirsty glanced around and also noticed a big tabby cat sleeping peacefully at the back of the barn on a small pile of hay.

Meanwhile, the goblin was perched on a large sack of animal feed, still holding Lucky. He was stroking her head gently.

"Well, at least he's being sweet to poor little Lucky," Lara whispered to Rachel and Kirsty.

"What shall we do now, girls? We need a plan!"

Suddenly there was a loud knock at the barn door.

"Let us in!" screeched one of the goblins outside. "Three of those annoying fairies have just flown into the barn – they want our magic cat!"

"Oh no!" Rachel groaned under her breath. The goblin holding Lucky looked up and scowled as he saw Lara and the girls fluttering overhead.

Clutching the cat tightly, he rushed over to the door and let his friends into the barn.

"Ha ha ha!" chuckled the third goblin triumphantly. "Now it's three against three!"

Lucky mewed anxiously, gazing helplessly at Lara and the girls with her big, emerald eyes.

"What are we going to do?" Rachel whispered.

Kirsty thought hard. How were they
going to get Lucky away from the
goblins and escape? She glanced around
the barn for inspiration and noticed
that the tabby cat had woken up and
was watching them all with interest.

Suddenly, Kirsty had an idea!

Double Bad Luck

"Lara!" Kirsty murmured quietly. "Could you turn the barn cat over there into a black cat, just like Lucky?"

"Of course!" Lara nodded.

"And please can you make me and Rachel our normal size again?" Kirsty added.

"In an instant!" Lara replied, her eyes twinkling. Hovering behind the girls so that the goblins couldn't see what she was doing, Lara pointed her wand at the tabby cat and sent a few fairy sparkles streaming towards it. Rachel's eyes widened as she saw the tabby's coat turn a gleaming jet black, just like Lucky's.

"Well, the cat doesn't seem to mind!" she whispered to Kirsty as the cat busily began to groom herself. "I think I've guessed what your plan is, Kirsty!"

"Let's hope it works," Kirsty said under her breath.

With another wave of Lara's wand, the girls grew back to their human size.

The goblin holding Lucky glared at them and took a step backwards. Immediately the other two rushed forwards, shielding him from Lara and the girls.

Kirsty ignored them. She walked over to the back of the barn and picked up the newly black cat. It was very friendly and nestled down in her arms, purring happily.

"Look, Rachel," Kirsty said, "we've found a *new* lucky cat!"

Rachel nodded. "Yes, and look how big it is," she replied. "That means our cat is *much* luckier than that little cat the silly goblins have!"

The goblin holding Lucky and the haystack goblin looked at each other in dismay. Then they both stared at the barn cat in Kirsty's arms, looking very envious.

"No, no, NO!" the third goblin announced loudly, hands on hips. "There's no way we're falling for *that* old trick again!"

Kirsty and Rachel exchanged a worried glance.

"We *always* end up swapping something magical for something useless," the goblin went on. "We're not swapping this time, so go away! We're taking this Magical Animal straight back to Jack Frost!"

"Girls, we can't let them leave!" Lara gasped.

Rachel and Kirsty leapt forward to grab Lucky, but the goblins had already scooted off. Dodging the girls, they ducked under a ladder leaning against the wall and headed for the barn door.

At that moment, an idea popped into Rachel's head.

"Oh!" She let out a loud gasp of horror. "I can't believe you just did that! You ran underneath a ladder, holding a black cat!"

The goblins stopped, looking rather nervous.

"So?" the one holding Lucky said rudely. "What's wrong with that?"

Rachel winked at Kirsty and Lara and then turned back to the goblins.

"Don't you know that's *doubly* unlucky?" she said, shaking her head.

"You've really gone and done it now!"

The goblins glanced at each other in dismay.

"Wh-what will happen now?" the third goblin gulped.

Kirsty shrugged. "Well, that's the thing with bad luck," she replied. "You never know *what's* going to happen!"

The goblins looked completely spooked.

"We don't want bad luck!" the one holding Lucky wailed. "How can we stop it?"

"Well, that's easy," Rachel said. "Just give us that black cat!"

"Yes, it's the only way to break the bad luck," Lara added. "And if you want to get some good luck back, there are lots of four-leaf clovers out in the field."

The goblins all frowned and stood
there in silence for a moment. Kirsty,
Lara and Rachel waited anxiously
to see what they would decide.

Would they give Lucky back?

—

Lucky at Last!

Finally, the three goblins nodded at each other.

"Let's go and get ourselves some good luck, and some for Jack Frost, too!" the goblin holding Lucky shouted. He put the little cat down on the floor and raced out of the barn with the other two goblins at his heels.

"They'll need all the good luck they can get when Jack Frost finds out they gave Lucky away!" Kirsty laughed.

"Yes, the goblins will need *hundreds* of lucky four-leaf clovers!" Rachel added with a smile.

Smiling from ear to ear, Lara held out her arms.

"Lucky!" she called.

The little cat's ears pricked up. She bounded up into the air and trotted straight towards Lara, shrinking down to fairy size as she did so.

"Oh it's so good to have you back, Lucky!" Lara exclaimed, gathering the cat into her arms and giving her a big hug.

"*Meow!*" Lucky agreed, purring as Rachel and Kirsty gently petted her tiny, silky head.

"Girls, this is all thanks to you," Lara announced gratefully. "I can't wait to get back to Fairyland and tell everyone how wonderful you both are! But first..."

She waved her wand and the cat in Kirsty's arms became a tabby once more. It blinked its eyes sleepily, then began purring as it spotted Lucky.

"My magic has replaced the haystacks in the farmyard, too," Lara told the girls. "And now Lucky and I must return to Fairyland."

"Oh no!" Rachel glanced at her watch, and then looked anxiously at Kirsty. "It's nearly twelve-thirty and we haven't even started on our orienteering expedition!"

"Don't worry, girls," Lara winked at them. "I have a feeling everything will work out just fine."

She twirled her wand and a shower of fairy sparkles tumbled down over herself and Lucky.

"Goodbye, girls, and thanks for everything!" Lara called as she and Lucky vanished in an instant.

"I was really worried that we weren't going to get Lucky back at all," Kirsty said, as she and Rachel hurried over to the barn door. "But we managed to fool the goblins in the end!"

"Yes, we were *lucky*!" Rachel laughed.

The girls walked out of the barn and then stopped in surprise. Outside stood Edward, their room-mates and all the other boys and girls taking part in the orienteering expedition.

"Well, it looks like everyone found our final meeting-place, then!" Edward remarked with a smile.

Kirsty and Rachel nodded, looking relieved.

"Lara said everything would work out fine – and it has!" Rachel whispered.

"We'll be doing some more orienteering after lunch," Edward went on, "but first – the surprise!" He pointed at the pretty little farmhouse. "The farmer and his wife have invited us to lunch, a roast dinner followed by fresh apple pie and ice cream! After that, they'll introduce us to some of the farm animals."

Everyone exclaimed in delight, and Kirsty and Rachel grinned at each other.

"This is going to be great," Kirsty said happily. "And we've already had lots of fun today with Lara and Lucky!"

"Yes, every day is exciting when we're having fairy adventures!" Rachel agreed. "I wonder which amazing Magical Animal we'll meet next?

The Magical Animal Fairies

Lara the Black Cat Fairy has got her
Magical Animal back! Now Rachel
and Kirsty must help...

Erin the Firebird Fairy

Ha! Ha!

Kirsty Tate held her breath, trying to keep her fingers steady on the camera as a little brown sparrow only a few steps away pecked at something on the ground. She was crouched at the edge of a woodland clearing, framed by leafy trees and bushes, with dappled sunlight streaming through. She pressed the button on top of the camera. Click! There – perfect.

"Brilliant," said her best friend, Rachel Walker, who was crouching next to Kirsty. She took her pencil and ticked off the sparrow's picture from a list she held on a clipboard. "That makes five birds we've found and photographed," she said, feeling pleased. "The sparrow, thrush, blackbird, robin and magpie. Just the blue tit to spot now, and we're done."

The two girls were spending a week of their spring holiday at an outdoors adventure camp. Today was Nature Day, and all the campers had been put in pairs and given a list of plants, animals or insects to track down and photograph. At the end of the day, they were going to gather around the campfire and share their discoveries with everyone.

Rachel and Kirsty sat on a fallen log to look at the birdwatcher's guidebook they had been given. Rachel flicked through until she found a page about the blue tit. "Here we are," she said, looking at the photograph. "So it's got a blue head, wings and tail, and a yellow chest. Well, that should be easy enough to spot."

"It says here that the blue tit is acrobatic and cheeky, and has a funny call: *tee, tee, tee,*" Kirsty said, reading aloud. She put her head on one side, listening hard. "I can't hear anything like that," she said after a moment.

"I'll have a look with these," Rachel said, picking up their binoculars and scanning the glade. She moved them around slowly, spotting clumps of primroses and nodding daffodils, but no blue tits. The only bird she could see was a robin perched on a tree stump. Rachel chuckled to herself as a joke suddenly popped into her head.

"What's so funny?" Kirsty wanted to know.

"I just thought of a joke," Rachel said. "Which bird steals from the rich to give to the poor?"

"I don't know," Kirsty replied.

"Robin Hood!" Rachel giggled.

Kirsty smiled. "I like that," she said. "I've got one too. Which bird tells the best jokes...?"

The Magical Animal Fairies

Win Rainbow Magic goodies!

In every book in the Magical Animal Fairies series
(books 71-77) there is a hidden picture of a pawprint with a secret
letter in it. Find all seven letters and re-arrange them to make
a special Magical Animal Fairies word, then send it to us. Each
month we will put the entries into a draw and select one winner
to receive a Rainbow Magic sparkly T-shirt and goody bag!

Send your entry on a postcard to Rainbow Magic Magical Animal
Fairies Competition, Orchard Books, 338 Euston Road, London
NW1 3BH. Australian readers should write to Hachette Children's
Books, Level 17/207 Kent Street, Sydney, NSW 2000.
New Zealand readers should write to Rainbow Magic Competition,
4 Whetu Place, Mairangi Bay, Auckland, NZ. Don't forget to
include your name and address. Only one entry per child.
Final draw: 30th April 2010.

Good luck!

Have you checked out the

website at:
www.rainbowmagic.co.uk

Look out for the
Green Fairies!

NICOLE
THE BEACH FAIRY
978-1-40830-474-7

ISABELLA
THE AIR FAIRY
978-1-40830-475-4

EDIE
THE GARDEN FAIRY
978-1-40830-476-1

CORAL
THE REEF FAIRY
978-1-40830-477-8

LILY
THE RAINFOREST FAIRY
978-1-40830-478-5

CARRIE
THE SNOW CAP FAIRY
978-1-40830-479-2

MILLY
THE RIVER FAIRY
978-1-40830-480-8

Available
September 2009